BRINGING THE RAIN TO KAPITI PLAIN

BRINGING THE RAIN TO KAPITI PLAIN

by Verna Aardema

illustrated by Beatriz Vidal

M

MACMILLAN CHILDREN'S BOOKS

Originally published in the USA by The Dial Press 1981
First published in Great Britain 1981 by
MACMILLAN CHILDREN'S BOOKS
a division of Macmillan Publishers Limited
London and Basingstoke
Associated companies throughout the world

Picturemac edition published 1986
British publication rights arranged with
Curtis Brown Ltd and The Dial Press

9 8 7 6

British Library Cataloguing in Publication Data
Aardema, Verna
    Bringing the rain to Kapiti plain.
    I. Title   II. Vidal. Beatriz
    811'.54 PS3551.A7/

    ISBN 0-333-35164-9

Printed in Hong Kong

For my librarian,
Bernice Houseward
V. A.

For my parents; for my teacher
B. V.

This is the great
    Kapiti Plain,
All fresh and green
    from the African rains—
A sea of grass for the
    ground birds to nest in,
And patches of shade for
    wild creatures to rest in;
With acacia trees for
    giraffes to browse on,
And grass for the herdsmen
    to pasture their cows on.

But one year the rains
    were so very belated,
That all of the big wild
    creatures migrated.
Then Ki-pat helped to end
    that terrible drought—
And this story tells
    how it all came about!

This is the cloud,
    all heavy with rain,
That shadowed the ground
    on Kapiti Plain.

This is the grass,
 all brown and dead,
That needed the rain
 from the cloud overhead—
The big, black cloud,
 all heavy with rain,
That shadowed the ground
 on Kapiti Plain.

These are the cows,
    all hungry and dry,
Who mooed for the rain
    to fall from the sky;
To green-up the grass,
    all brown and dead,
That needed the rain
    from the cloud overhead—
The big, black cloud,
    all heavy with rain,
That shadowed the ground
    on Kapiti Plain.

This is Ki-pat,
    who watched his herd
As he stood on one leg,
    like the big stork bird;
Ki-pat, whose cows
    were so hungry and dry,
They mooed for the rain
    to fall from the sky;
To green-up the grass,
    all brown and dead,
That needed the rain
    from the cloud overhead—
The big, black cloud,
    all heavy with rain,
That shadowed the ground
    on Kapiti Plain.

This is the eagle
     who dropped a feather,
A feather that helped
     to change the weather.
It fell near Ki-pat,
     who watched his herd
As he stood on one leg,
     like the big stork bird;
Ki-pat, whose cows
     were so hungry and dry,
They mooed for the rain
     to fall from the sky;
To green-up the grass,
     all brown and dead,
That needed the rain
     from the cloud overhead—
The big, black cloud,
     all heavy with rain,
That shadowed the ground
     on Kapiti Plain.

This is the arrow
  Ki-pat put together,
With a slender stick
  and an eagle feather;
From the eagle who happened
  to drop a feather,
A feather that helped
  to change the weather.

It fell near Ki-pat,
    who watched his herd
As he stood on one leg,
    like the big stork bird;
Ki-pat, whose cows
    were so hungry and dry,
They mooed for the rain
    to fall from the sky;
To green-up the grass,
    all brown and dead,
That needed the rain
    from the cloud overhead—
The big, black cloud,
    all heavy with rain,
That shadowed the ground
    on Kapiti Plain.

This is the bow,
    so long and strong,
And strung with a string,
    a leather thong;
A bow for the arrow
    Ki-pat put together,
With a slender stick
    and an eagle feather;
From the eagle who happened
    to drop a feather,
A feather that helped
    to change the weather.

It fell near Ki-pat,
  who watched his herd
As he stood on one leg,
  like the big stork bird;
Ki-pat, whose cows
  were so hungry and dry,
They mooed for the rain
  to fall from the sky;
To green-up the grass,
  all brown and dead,
That needed the rain
  from the cloud overhead—
The big, black cloud,
  all heavy with rain,
That shadowed the ground
  on Kapiti Plain.

This was the shot
  that pierced the cloud
And loosed the rain
  with thunder LOUD!
A shot from the bow,
  so long and strong,
And strung with a string,
  a leather thong;
A bow for the arrow
  Ki-pat put together,
With a slender stick
  and an eagle feather;
From the eagle who happened
  to drop a feather,
A feather that helped
  to change the weather.

It fell near Ki-pat,
     who watched his herd
As he stood on one leg,
     like the big stork bird;
Ki-pat, whose cows
     were so hungry and dry,
They mooed for the rain
     to fall from the sky;
To green-up the grass,
     all brown and dead,
That needed the rain
     from the cloud overhead—
The big, black cloud,
     all heavy with rain,
That shadowed the ground
     on Kapiti Plain.

So the grass grew green,
and the cattle fat!
And Ki-pat got a wife
and a little Ki-pat—

Who tends the cows now,
    and shoots down the rain,
When black clouds shadow
    Kapiti Plain.

About the Author

Verna Aardema is a highly acclaimed storyteller and the author of many books of African folktales. Her most recent book for Dial, *Who's in Rabbit's House?*, illustrated by Leo and Diane Dillon, was an American Library Association Notable Children's Book and a *School Library Journal* Best Book of the Year, 1977. *Why Mosquitoes Buzz in People's Ears*, also illustrated by the Dillons, was awarded the Caldecott Medal in 1976 and was chosen as an American Library Association Notable Children's Book, as was a third Aardema-Dillon collaboration, *Behind the Back of the Mountain*.

Ms. Aardema was born in New Era, Michigan, and received her degree in journalism from Michigan State University. She now lives in Muskegon, Michigan, with her husband, Dr. Joel Vugteveen.

About the Artist

Beatriz Vidal was born in Argentina and received her Bachelor of Arts from Córdoba University. She has studied art with Ilonka Karasz, and her illustrations have appeared on UNICEF cards and publications including *Vogue* and *Woman's Day*.

Ms. Vidal currently lives in New York City. This is her first children's book.

About the Tale

This tale was discovered in Kenya, Africa, more than seventy years ago by the famous anthropologist Sir Claud Hollis. Sir Claud camped near a Nandi village and learned the native language from two young boys. He learned riddles and proverbs from the Nandi children, and most of the folktales from the Chief Medicine Man. This tale reminded Sir Claud of a cumulative nursery rhyme he had loved as a boy in England, one also familiar to us—"The House That Jack Built." So he called the story "The Nandi House That Jack Built" and included it in his book *The Nandi: Their Language and Folklore*, published in 1909. Verna Aardema has brought the original story closer to the English nursery rhyme by putting in a cumulative refrain and giving the tale the rhythm of "The House That Jack Built."